FIRE TRUCK Dreams

by Sharon Chriscoe

illustrated by
Dave Mottram

RP|KIDS
PHILADELPHIA

Running Press Kids
Hachette Book Group
1290 Avenue of the Americas, New York, NY 10104
www.runningpress.com/rpkids
@RP_Kids

Printed in China

First Edition: October 2018

Published by Running Press Kids, an imprint of Perseus Books, LLC,
a subsidiary of Hachette Book Group, Inc.
The Running Press Kids name and logo is a trademark of the Hachette Book Group.

The Hachette Speakers Bureau provides a wide range of authors for speaking events.
To find out more, go to www.hachettespeakersbureau.com or call (866) 376-6591.

The publisher is not responsible for websites (or their content)
that are not owned by the publisher.

Print book cover and interior design by T.L. Bonaddio.

Library of Congress Control Number: 2017933538

ISBNs: 978-0-7624-6285-8 (hardcover), 978-0-7624-9295-4 (ebook),
978-0-7624-9294-7 (ebook), 978-0-7624-6286-5 (ebook)

1010

10 9 8 7 6 5 4 3 2 1

A siren turns off. The sun fades away.
Fire truck is drained. He's had a big day.

From raging brush fires
to kittens in trees,

he's kept the town safe from danger with ease.

He looks to the homes and then to the park.
All quiet and safe, asleep in the dark.

His headlights turn on. His ladder's locked tight.

He blinks and he yawns,
then whispers,
"Goodnight."

Off to the station to shower and clean—
bumper to taillight and all in between.

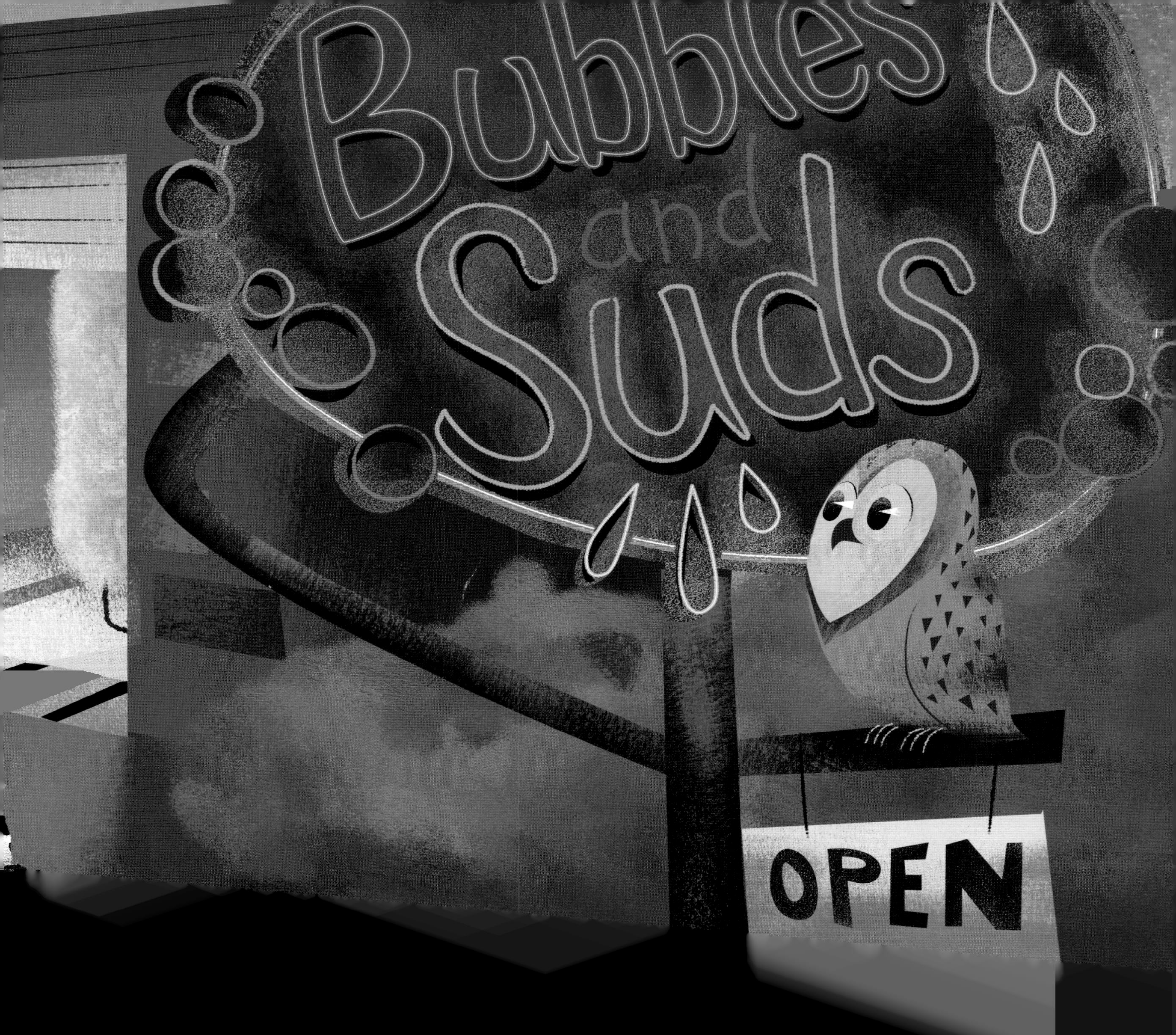
Bubbles and Suds
OPEN

He washes and scrubs. He shines up his bells.

His nose starts to twitch from rich, sudsy smells.

All shiny and fresh
his tummy draws tight.
Then echoes a growl
across the black night.

GROW

He pulls to the pump. He opens his cap.

He swishes and swigs, then makes one last lap.

His eyelids grow heavy. It's time to head back.

He chooses his book.
His flashers *click-clack*.

He backs in his bay. His bucket pulls close.

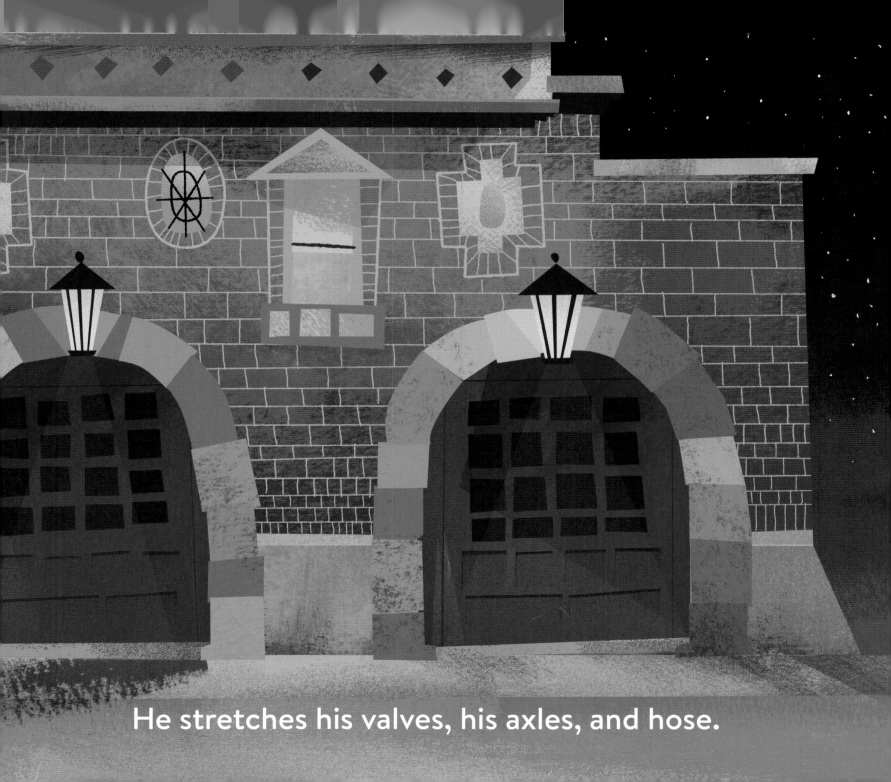

He stretches his valves, his axles, and hose.

An icy wind blasts. He shivers a chill.
He closes his book and clenches his grill.

He turns on the heat and nestles in tight.
The stars twinkle low. The moon casts its light.

His pressures release. He lets off some steam.
His hoses deflate as he drifts to a dream.

Alarms start to blare. There's trouble nearby!
His grill sniffs the air. There's smoke in the sky!

His sirens call out. He zooms to the sand.
He finds a campfire that got out of hand.

A hero's parade to end his big day.
The children salute him. Hip Hip Hooray!
The campers all cheer! They offer him s'mores.
Sweet treats fill his dream. He grins as he snores.